Rose and Riley Come and Go

Jane Cutler

Pictures by **Thomas F. Yezerski**

Farrar Straus Giroux

New York

For Dave and Luz
—J.C.
To Rob and Karen
—T.F.Y.

Text copyright © 2005 by Jane Cutler
Illustrations copyright © 2005 by Thomas F. Yezerski
All rights reserved
Distributed in Canada by Douglas & McIntyre Publishing Group
Color separations by Chroma Graphics PTE Ltd.
Printed in the United States of America by Phoenix Color Corporation
Designed by Jay Colvin
First edition, 2005
10 9 8 7 6 5 4 3 2 1

www.fsgkidsbooks.com

Library of Congress Cataloging-in-Publication Data
Cutler, Jane.
    Rose and Riley come and go / Jane Cutler ; pictures by Thomas F. Yezerski.—
1st ed.
        p. cm.
    Summary: Relates the outdoor adventures of two good friends as they
collect seashells, photograph wildflowers, and listen to the songs of a backyard
mockingbird.
    ISBN-13: 978-0-374-36341-3
    ISBN-10: 0-374-36341-2
    [1. Best friends—Fiction. 2. Friendship—Fiction. 3. Nature study—Fiction.]
I. Yezerski, Thomas, ill. II. Title.

PZ7.C985Rr 2005
[E]—dc22

                                                                    2004043332

Contents

The Seashell

Rose and her friend Riley
were going to the beach.
"We will need water to drink," said Rose.
"And *sand*-wiches!" said Riley.
"Yes," Rose said. "What kind?"
"Sand sandwiches, Rose," said Riley.
"We can make them at the beach."
"Riley," said Rose, "I am making
a cheese sandwich. Do you want me
to make one for you, too?"
"Rose, you are not in a good mood,"
said Riley.
"I will be in a good mood
when we get to the beach," said Rose.

Rose made cheese sandwiches.

She put the sandwiches and the water

into a beach bag.

Then she got hats, a blanket, a bucket,

a shovel, and an umbrella.

"We are ready to go," said Rose.

"One more thing!" Riley said.

Riley got a picture of a seashell.

The shell was big. It was pink.

It was perfect.

"Today I am going to look for a seashell

like this one," Riley said.

"I have never seen one like that," said Rose.

"If we take the picture, we will know

what to look for," said Riley.

Rose and Riley found a place to sit.

They put down the blanket.

They put up the umbrella.

They put on their hats and went to look
for a big, pink, perfect seashell.

They saw water. They saw waves.

They saw seaweed.

They saw beach grass.

They saw many small, fast birds.
But they did not see a big, pink,
perfect seashell.

They went back to the blanket.

"Now *I* am not in a good mood," said Riley.

"I am going to rest."

"I am going to walk some more," said Rose.

She walked down to the water.

She found many seashells.

They were small.

They were black and white and brown.

Most of them were broken.

But they felt good to hold.

They smelled like the sea.

And they were all around.

Rose found some she liked

and put them in the bucket.

Then she went back to show Riley.

"Look, Riley," she said.

"I have found some nice seashells."

Rose took the shells out of the bucket.

"Those shells are not big," Riley said.

"They are not pink.

They are not perfect."

"You are right, they are not perfect," said Rose,

"but they are real."

"They feel good to hold," said Riley.

"They smell like the sea," said Rose.

"You can put them in your pocket," said Riley.

"You can find them all around," said Rose.

"A real seashell is different
  from a picture of a seashell,
  isn't it, Rose?" said Riley.

"It is, Riley," said Rose.

Wildflowers

"It is a nice day," said Rose,
"a nice day to go to the woods
  to hunt for wildflowers."
"Hunt for *Wild* Flowers?" said Riley.
"Yes," said Rose. "There should be a lot
  of wildflowers out now."

The thought of seeing even one
Wild Flower scared Riley.

"I am not sure I want to do that," Riley said.

"That is okay," said Rose.

"I will go on a wildflower hunt by myself."

Riley jumped up.

"No!" he cried. "I will go with you!"

"Okay," said Rose. "I will wait for you outside."

Riley got his bat.

He got a scary mask.

"Why are you bringing
a bat and a scary mask?" asked Rose.

"In case we see Wild Flowers,"
answered Riley.

"I am taking my camera," said Rose.

"Why?" asked Riley.

"In case we see wildflowers," answered Rose.

23

Rose and Riley walked in the woods.

Rose looked for wildflowers.

Riley watched out for Wild Flowers.

Rose felt happy.

Riley felt afraid.

Soon Rose said, "I see one!"

Riley put on his scary mask.

He held up his bat. "Where?" he cried.

"Right there, peeking out from behind that rock.

A purple wildflower."

Riley took off his mask.

He went closer.

He saw a little purple flower.

He put his mask back on. He held up his bat.

He looked all around.

"What is the matter?" asked Rose.

"That flower is so little,

it must be a baby Wild Flower," said Riley.

"The mother Wild Flower

and the father Wild Flower must be nearby!"

Rose thought Riley was joking.

She took a picture of the flower.

"Riley, do you know what
   you are really afraid of?" she asked.
"Of course I do," said Riley.
"What?" asked Rose.
"I told you, I am afraid
   of big, scary, Wild Flowers!"

"But wildflowers are small," said Rose.

"And they are not at all scary."

"They are Wild, aren't they?" said Riley.

"Yes, they are wild."

"That means they are scary," said Riley.

"It means they are bad."

"No," said Rose. "It means nobody planted them.

It means nobody takes care of them."

Rose stopped to take a picture

of some tiny red flowers.

"Do these flowers look scary?" she asked.

"Do they look bad?"

Riley looked at the tiny red flowers.

They did not look scary or bad.

Riley took off his mask.

He dragged his bat.

Soon Rose and Riley came

to a field full of yellow flowers.

The yellow flowers looked like a soft yellow rug.
Rose smiled.

"Go and stand in the field, Riley," she said.

"I will take a picture of you

with all those pretty yellow wildflowers."

"Are you sure it is safe?" asked Riley.

"I am sure," said Rose.

Brave Riley stood out in the field
surrounded by Wild Flowers.
Rose took his picture.

The Mockingbird

Many birds started to sing in Riley's yard.

They sang in the morning.

They sang in the afternoon.

The birds even sang at night.

At first, Riley was happy.

"Many birds live in my yard," he told Rose.

"They sing all the time."

But soon, Riley was tired.

"Too many birds live in my yard.

They sing all the time.

I cannot sleep at night."

Rose came to Riley's house.

She heard birds singing.

"How many birds live in your yard, Riley?"

Rose asked.

"Ten," Riley said.

"Have you seen ten different birds?" Rose asked.

"No," said Riley. "I have not seen ten birds.

I have seen only one bird."

"Then what makes you think

there are ten?" asked Rose.

"I counted the songs they sing," said Riley.

"Listen. You can count them, too."

Rose listened. Here is what she heard.

Whit-Whistle-Churr-Pwee-Twee-

Shree-Heep-Peep-Cheep-See!

"I hear ten different songs!" said Rose.

"That is what I said," said Riley.

"I want to see the birds," said Rose.

"I do not want to see them," said Riley.

"I just want them to go away."

Rose went into the yard.

Up at the top of the apple tree,

she saw one little bird,

singing with all its might.

Whit-Whistle-Churr-Pwee-Twee-

Shree-Heep-Peep-Cheep-See!

"Riley," Rose said. "You do not have ten
birds living in your yard.

You have one bird living in your yard."

"But, Rose," said Riley,

"I counted ten different songs."

"Yes," said Rose. "That is because

the bird in your yard is a mockingbird."

"A mocking bird?" said Riley.

"You mean there is a bird in my yard

that is making fun of me?"

"Mocking does not just mean

making fun of something," said Rose.

"It means copying, too.

The mockingbird is copying

the songs of other birds."

"You mean one bird is sounding

like ten different birds?" said Riley.

"Yes!" said Rose. "See?"

She pointed to the one little bird, singing away.

"It has nothing to do with you."

"It has something to do with me," said Riley.

"It is in my yard. It is in my apple tree.

It is keeping me awake at night."

"Yes," said Rose.

"I do not like to be kept awake, Rose. Do you?"

"Birds do not keep me awake at night, Riley."

"Even mockingbirds that sing ten different

songs?" asked Riley.

"Even mockingbirds that sing ten different

songs," said Rose.

"Then I will sleep at your house
and you can sleep here.
Will that be all right, Rose?" asked Riley.
"That will be just fine, Riley," said Rose.